For my parents
who have always
supported me

www.mascotbooks.com

Joanna Banana

For more information, please contact:

Mascot Books
620 Herndon Parkway #320
Herndon, VA 20170
info@mascotbooks.com

Library of Congress Control Number: 2018914682

CPSIA Code: PRT0119A
ISBN-13: 978-1-64307-032-2

Printed in the United States

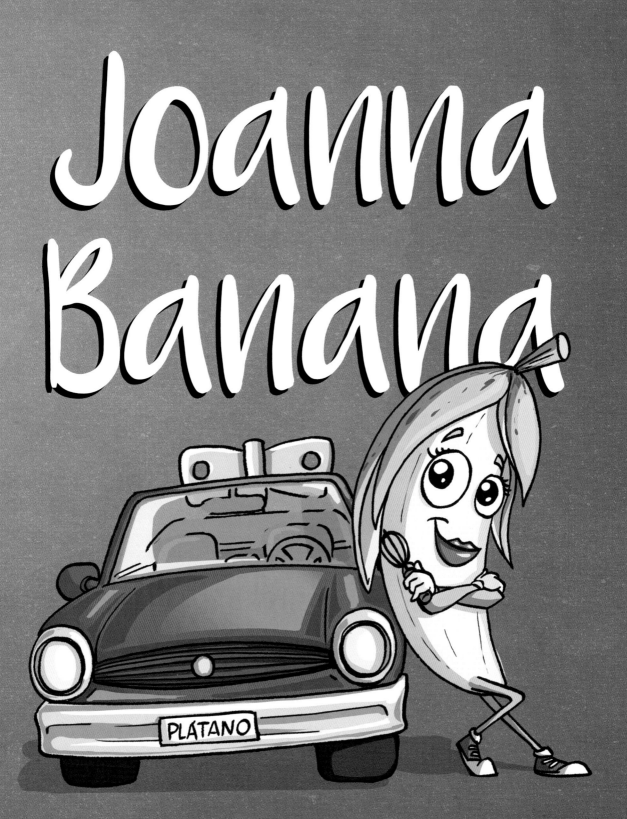

Joanna Banana

Written by **Megan Mears**

Illustrated by **Walter Policelli**

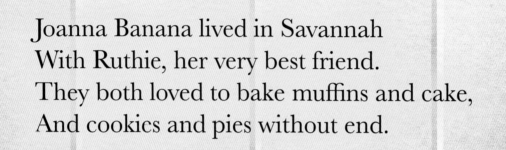

Joanna Banana lived in Savannah
With Ruthie, her very best friend.
They both loved to bake muffins and cake,
And cookies and pies without end.

And when Ruthie was sad, or just feeling bad,
Joanna knew just what to do.
She'd go to the kitchen and get down to mixin'
Banana bread muffins for two.

Mix bananas and nutmeg with butter and egg,
And stir while the oven is heating.
Add sugar and flour, then bake half an hour,
Till muffins are ready for eating.

Muffins so yummy and warm in your tummy,
They'd brighten up Ruthie's whole day.
Chase them down with a smile and then after a while,
The blues were all washed away.

But one day while playing, Ruthie kept saying,
"My tummy hurts, I think I'm sick."

Jo pulled out her recipe, whipped up her specialty,
But muffins weren't doing the trick.

Ruthie's mom made a call and in no time at all,
The doctor was able to see her.
After samples and tests, and a thorough inquest,
He said, "The results are quite clear."

"The reason your tummy is feeling so crummy,
My dear, there's just no disputin',
The pastries you eat are filled up with wheat,
And it seems you're allergic to gluten!"

"No more muffins?" cried Jo, "This is awful, oh no!"
And Ruthie looked simply deflated.
"Not to worry," said Doc, "this is not a roadblock,
You'll just have to get more creative."

"I'm on it," said Jo, "Someone must know
A way to make bread you can eat."
And Joanna Banana drove to Indiana
In search of an alternate treat.

As she drove through the plains, passing miles of grains,
She thought she heard distant moos.
And when she came near, she saw cows in the clear,
Playing checkers and tossing horseshoes.

"What are you doing?" Jo asked through the mooing,
"Have you finished your milking already?"
"We don't milk anymore," said a cow keeping score,
"On account of it botherin' poor Freddie."

"See, the farmer's son Fred was laid up in bed,
His stomach blown up like a berry,
But the big bloated mass turned out to be gas–
Seems that Freddie's allergic to dairy."

"So his mom and his dad took the milk that they had
And replaced it, quick as a breeze,
With milk made from rice, which made Fred feel nice,
Now we spend our days as we please!"

How delightful, Jo thought. *I like that a lot–
Swapping rice milk to combat the tootin'.*
So Joanna Banana drove on to Montana
To find something to swap for the gluten.

As she left the prairie, still thinking of dairy,
She happened upon a small brood
Of beautiful hens dancing jigs in their pens;
They seemed in a joyful mood.

"Say!" shouted Jo, "I'm curious to know
Why you aren't on your roosts laying eggs."
"We don't lay anymore since our poor Eleanor
Got hives on her arms and her legs."

"Eggs gave her a rash, so quick as a flash,
Her Nana gave them the toss.
And now when she bakes, she makes Ellie's cakes
With a spoonful of applesauce."

"Smart!" said Joanna, "I'm so glad her Nana
Was able to make a quick switch.
And Ellie can still eat up her fill
Of cupcakes that don't make her itch!"

All she was learning was stewing and churning
As Jo headed back home's way,
She drove through Texarkana and then Lou'siana,
And ended up down by the bay.

Eggs and dairy can be made less scary
By simply substitutin',
So what could she choose that's easy to use
To take the place of the gluten?

"I think," Jo said, "the answer to bread
Might require some tropical zest."
So Joanna Banana sailed off to Havana
To continue her ingredient quest.

She combed through the town and searched all around,
Then went to the forest to scour
For something delicious, and also nutritious,
To turn into gluten-free flour.

She saw pineapples, cherries, and bright red strawberries,
Though nothing that looked right for bread.
But as she was sitting and thinking of quitting,
A coconut fell on her head!

"Pardon me," said the fruit who was really quite cute,
"I'm ripe now, so if you're inclined,
Just put me to use and squeeze out my juice,
I assure you I truly don't mind."

"I didn't know," said a shocked-looking Jo,
"That you had such sweet juicing power."
"And pulp you can shred," the coconut said,
"And grind into sweet-tasting flour."

"I'm pleased as can be!" Jo shouted with glee,
Through a grin very silly and toothy,
"And I know how to make flour now
To put in the muffins for Ruthie!"

"Come, coconut friend, my quest's at an end!"
Said Jo, as they set out for sea.
Coconut and Banana sailed home to Savannah
And worked on a new recipe.

They measured and mixed, they added and nixed,
Until they made muffins most fine.
And Ruthie ate cake without tummy ache,
And their pastries and pies were divine!

About the Author

Megan Mears loves reading, traveling, and especially baking. When she's not working, Megan enjoys trying out new recipes. In fact, she was inspired to write *Joanna Banana* while experimenting with a variety of different cooking styles. She's lived all over the US, but is currently refining her high elevation baking skills in Colorado.

Joanna Banana is Megan's first children's book.

About the Illustrator

Walter Policelli was born in Buenos Aires in 1983 and has been drawing almost since then. His degree in social communication along with his creativity and his innate love for drawing has shaped him through the years as an awarded illustrator. He is fond of illustrating children's books but has also worked on a wide variety of other types of projects as well, including video games and scientific publications. He lives with his wife and son in a small town close to Iguazú Falls.